Santa's Elf

igloobooks

One Christmas at the North Pole, the elves were busy tapping,
using their little hammers to get presents ready for wrapping.

There were toys galore, like fancy dolls and many a cuddly teddy.
"Keep going, little elves!" said Santa. "Make sure those gifts are ready."

Suddenly, Santa's good-o-meter began flashing and making a noise.
"Uh-oh," said the elves and they all stopped building the toys.

The good-o-meter buzzed and beeped, then lit up from zero to ten.
"Oh, dear," said Santa, "it looks like Little Bear is being naughty again."

Far away, Little Bear was eating sweets before tea.

Then, he threw a snowball at his sister,

thinking no one else would see.

"Hmm," said Santa, gravely, "if that bear doesn't behave himself, he won't get any presents, so I'm sending him an elf."

Santa sent a Christmas elf to help Little Bear behave.
He put him on a shooting star and sent him off with a wave.

SANTA'S WORKSHOP

"Hello," said the elf, to Bear's surprise, "we need to have a chat."
He straightened his little jacket and jingled his jingle bell hat.

"Now then, Little Bear," said the elf, "Santa's been watching you."

"He knows you've been playing tricks and stealing candies, too."

"It's very important at Christmas to try to be at your best.
There won't be any presents, if you fail the good behavior test."

"Don't worry," said the elf, "all you have to do is follow me."
Then, he showed Little Bear how to decorate the Christmas tree.

The elf helped Little Bear to mix and stir and make
a sparkly frosted snowman, to go on a Christmas cake.

Little Bear listened to the elf and soon all the work was done.

"Wow!" cried the happy little bear. "That was so much fun!"

"If you tidy up," said the elf, "and put everything away,
Santa and Mommy will see you've been a very good bear today."

Soon, the house was clean. Mommy couldn't believe her eyes.
"Oh, Little Bear," she said. "What a wonderful surprise!"

"Well done," said the elf.
"Your behavior is much better.
Maybe you should sit down
and write Santa Claus a letter."

The elf called for the star to take him home on Christmas Eve.
"Goodbye," he said to Little Bear, just as he was about to leave.

"Always remember to be kind, and be your very best self...

"... because not too far away, watching, will be a Christmas elf."

Back home at the North Pole, the elf was feeling happy.
"Good job!" said Santa. "Let's load the sleigh, and make it snappy!"